Collins

D1584859

THE PASSENGER

D1584860

Dan Tunstall

Illustrated by

9030 00007 3464 0

Chapter 1

I've finally got to the front of the line. Even from here, I can see the bus is packed. It's always full on a Saturday evening. I check my watch. Nearly 5:30. I've been shopping in Renton all afternoon. Now I'm going home. It's October and it's already getting dark.

I get my ID card out, ready to show the driver.
I shake my head. The photo was taken two or
three years ago. I had a mega-dodgy haircut back
then. A black, spiky bog brush. I could be Simon
Cowell's secret son. It's not a good look. My hair's
a lot better now. Longer, sort of shaggy. A bit
skater-dude.

BAY 14

Bus Station
Penworth
Lenby

3

Soon, I'm stepping onto the bus. It's good to be out of the cold. I hold up my ID.

"Half single to Lenby, please," I say.

The driver is a bloke in his fifties. He's got greasy, grey hair and a big, saggy face like an unhappy bloodhound. He looks at my card, then looks at me. He nods slowly and taps the details into the ticket machine.

"£1.45," he says.

I hand over two pound coins and wait for my change. With my ticket in my hand, I head along the gangway. There aren't any spare seats. I puff out my cheeks. It's a long trip home and it looks like I'll have to stand. I've almost given up hope. But then I see, over to the left, two empty spaces. I can't believe my luck. I won't even have to share.

Quick as a flash, I'm in there. I put my shopping bags down and stretch my legs out under the seat in front.

The bus is about to leave the station. The doors close and the driver starts the engine, pulling out of the bay. Suddenly there's a hiss. I look up. The doors have opened again and one last passenger has got on. A tall lad in baggy jeans and a green hoodie. He's black with his hair in neat cornrows. He flashes his bus pass and starts looking for a seat. There's only one place left. Next to me.

The kid comes across and sits down. He looks a couple of years older than me. Sixteen or seventeen, I reckon. He's got lines shaved into his eyebrows and a scar on his right cheek. A gold stud glints in his left ear. He seems to be panting, out of breath. Like he's been running. There are little beads of sweat on his top lip. He looks at me and nods. But he says nothing.

It takes a while for the bus to get out of town. I wipe steam off the window and stare into the darkness outside, watching shops and houses swish by. Ten minutes in and the lad next to me has started humming to himself and drumming his fingers on his knees. It's making me feel edgy. I shift from side to side in my seat.

I get my phone out, check my messages.
Nothing new. I'm putting the phone away when
the kid beside me turns round.

"All right, mate?" he says. He holds out his
hand. "I'm Mikey."

My mind goes blank.

The hand is still hanging in midair.

I blink, waking myself up.

"Sorry, mate." I grab Mikey's hand and shake. "I'm Matt."

"Good to meet you, man." Mikey lets go and points to my bags. "Been shopping?"

"Yeah. Didn't get very much though. Couple of T-shirts. I was looking for some jeans but there wasn't anything I liked."

"I know what you mean," Mikey says. "It's hard to find stuff sometimes, isn't it?"

"Yeah. It's like there's too much choice. So have you been shopping, too?"

"No." Mikey rubs the back of his neck. "I had some things to do. Some people to see."

"Right," I say, nodding. "Anyway, I'm going back home now. Lenby."

Mikey smiles.

"I know Lenby. I live near there. Penworth."

"Oh, Penworth," I say. "Just down the road."

I sink back into my seat. I'm not feeling edgy any more. In fact, I'm feeling pretty relaxed now. A little flicker of guilt goes through me. When he first got on the bus, I thought Mikey was a bit scary. But he's not scary at all. He's okay.

Chapter 2

Once me and Mikey have started chatting, we never seem to stop. For the next twenty minutes it's like we're old mates, catching up. At first it's just clothes, music, TV, football, girls. It turns out we've got quite a bit in common. We're having a good laugh. But then Mikey begins to get more serious. It seems he needs to get stuff off his chest.

13

"You know, there are some bad things going down in Renton these days." His voice is suddenly quieter.

"Yeah?" My own voice drops down a notch or two. "What sort of things do you mean?"

Mikey glances around, checking that no one is listening to what he's going to say. He takes a deep breath.

"Gangs. Weapons. Violence. Pretty heavy, some of it."

I don't know much about gangs, but I've heard the rumours.

"I suppose it can be a bit dodgy in town at night," I say.

"It's not just dodgy at night. Some parts of Renton are like a warzone any time of the day. It's scary, man." His voice is not much more than a whisper now.

I nod. There's nothing I can really say.

Mikey checks up and down the bus one more time, then turns towards me. He looks right into my eyes. "You're not mixed up in any gangs, are you?"

I shake my head.

"Take my advice," he says. "Keep it that way. Kids nowadays – even the young ones – you never know what they're carrying. Knives. Guns. And they'll use them. They don't care about anything. It's crazy."

"Yeah. I make sure I stay out of all of that."

Mikey looks into my eyes again, making sure I'm telling the truth. He seems pleased by what he can see.

"That's good, man," he says finally. "These lads, they don't think what they're getting into. All this 'respect' rubbish. Sometimes it's better to just walk away."

My mobile buzzes. I reach into my pocket.

"Just a second."

I take out my phone and turn it over in my hand. I touch the screen and it springs into life. I've got a text from Mum. I open it up and start to read.

heard on radio there's been stabbing in renton. young lad been killed, attacker got away. r u ok? where r u now? mum x.

I blink, looking at the text again to make sure I've read it right. I have. A kid has been stabbed to death in Renton. It's hard to believe. Strange, too. We were just talking about that sort of stuff.

I know Mum will be worried. I need to let her know I'm okay. I click the Reply button.

hi mum i'm fine. on bus, home soon, matt x.

When the message is sent, I put my phone back in my pocket. Then I turn to Mikey again.

"Sorry about that, mate. Text from my mum. Some kid was killed in Renton. You know what mums are like." I smile. "She still thinks I'm five, I reckon."

Mikey says nothing. He runs his hand across his hair. Then he looks down at his trainers.

For some reason, I look down, too. Mikey's trainers are box-fresh Nikes. They're as white as new snow. White leather, white laces, white soles. But something on the right shoe catches my eye. It's a tiny circle. The size of a five-pence piece. It's bright, bright red. Blood.

My breath sticks in my throat. I sit up in my seat. The edgy feeling from earlier is back. But it's ten times worse now. And then I spot something else. A dark patch on the sleeve of Mikey's hoodie. More blood.

I'm frozen to the spot. My heart is thumping against my ribs. Suddenly, horribly, things are linking up in my mind. The kid killed in Renton. Why Mikey was sweaty and worn out when he got on the bus. Why he'd been running. The things he's been talking about. Gangs. Knives. The blood on his trainers and his hoodie.

All these links can only mean one thing. It's almost too shocking to be true. But it has to be.

I'm sitting next to a murderer.

23

Chapter 3

My heart is beating so fast it feels like it's going to jump out of my chest. I try to look at Mikey. I try to think of something to say. But I can't. Again and again, I find myself staring at the red stains on Mikey's trainers and hoodie.

We've been talking for ages. Now there's nothing. Just the sound of the engine, rising and falling as the driver changes gears.

What makes things worse is that Mikey seems to know that something is wrong. He's sweating again, checking his watch.

Two more minutes and we're coming into Penworth. The village bus stop is looming out of the darkness. Mikey stands up and rings the bell, letting the driver know he wants to get off. He turns towards me.

"I'm glad we talked, man," he says. He holds out his hand.

At first, I can't move. Finally, I stretch out my hand and we shake.

There's an odd look in Mikey's eyes. Sad, somehow.

"Time to go," he says.

Before I can say anything, he's heading for the exit.

The doors open and close and the driver revs the engine. I try to catch a final sight of Mikey. He's still at the bus stop. He's just standing there, staring up at the night sky. Then the bus pulls away and he's gone.

My head is spinning at a million miles an hour. All sorts of questions are swirling through my brain. What should I do? Call the police? Speak to the teachers at school on Monday? I've got a duty to report what I know, but it's dodgy being a grass.

27

If the cops knock on Mikey's door, he's going to know who it was that tipped them off. What if they don't charge him? He's going to come looking for me.

I feel helpless. I wish there was someone I could talk to. There's Mum, of course. But Mum just won't get it. Parents never do. I need to speak to someone my own age. Someone who would understand how things really are.

There's no time to think about that though. The bus is already coming into the middle of Lenby. I'm off at the next stop.

I pick up my bags and make my way to the front. The bus slows down and the doors hiss open. I'm stepping onto the pavement when someone pokes me in the ribs. I almost jump. Spinning round, I see it's Jess, my mate from school.

29

"Hi, Matt," she says. "Did you hear about the kid who got stabbed in Renton?"

"Yeah. My mum texted."

Jess rolls her eyes.

"You never think something like that could happen so close to home."

I nod. I look at Jess. I wanted someone to talk to. This is my chance.

But it's only a short walk from the bus stop to her house. If I'm going to say anything, it's now or never. I open my mouth and the words start tumbling out.

"Jess. You'll think I'm making this up. But I'm not. You know that lad who was sitting next to me, the one who got off in Penworth? Well, he's got to have something to do with that stabbing. He had blood on his trainers and his hoodie."

Jess looks at me like I've gone mad.

My heart sinks.

"See," I say. "I knew you wouldn't believe me."

Jess pulls her bag up onto her shoulder.

"I don't know what I can say."

"Well, what do you think I should do?" I ask.

Jess shakes her head.

"Matt, I watched you get on at Renton bus station. I was sitting at the back with Chris. I could see you all the way home. There was no one next to you."

I laugh. It's not me that's mad. It's Jess.

"What?" I say. "You didn't spot him then? Big kid, green hoodie? How could you not see him?"

"You must have been dreaming," Jess says.

33

I'm not laughing any more. I wasn't dreaming on the bus. I was wide awake. There's a sick feeling in my gut. Something isn't right.

"You're not kidding, are you?" I ask. "You're not just messing with my head?"

We're at Jess's house now.

Jess holds her hands out wide.

"Honest. I swear on my life. The seat next to you was empty. You were on your own."

Chapter 4

I set off down the street. Every few steps, I take a huge gulp of freezing night air. I'm trying to clear my head, but it's no good. My brain is spinning more than ever. Nothing makes sense. Talking to Jess hasn't made anything better. It's just made it worse.

Soon, I'm home. I walk down the path to the front door and let myself in.

Inside the house, the smell of cooking is wafting from the kitchen. Mum's been baking. She's waiting in the hall, looking stressed. As soon as she sees me, her eyes light up. Before I've even closed the door, she throws her arms round my neck and gives me a kiss on the cheek.

"Oh, Matt," she says. "I was so scared when I heard about that poor boy in Renton."

I pull back, dumping my bags on the floor. I try to smile, but I know it looks fake.

"Chill, Mum," I say. "Nothing to worry about. I'm fine."

Mum tilts her head to one side. She narrows her eyes.

"Are you sure you're fine, love?" she asks. "You don't look well."

"Yeah, I'm okay. I just had a very weird trip home."

Mum looks puzzled.

"Weird? In what way?"

I shrug.

"It's hard to explain," I say. "Anyway, is there any more news about the stabbing?"

Mum nods.

"Yes. I've had the TV on all afternoon. People passing by tried to help, but it was too late. The lad died at the scene. Right by the bus station, in one of the side streets."

I cut in.

BREAKING NEWS TEEN KILLED IN RENTON

"What about the kid that did it? Have they got him now?"

Mum shakes her head.

"He ran away. Nobody could catch him."

"Are there any details about what he looked like?" I'm trying to keep my voice steady, but I need to know the facts. All the facts. "Anything about what he was wearing?"

Mum shakes her head again.

"No. Nothing like that. They're saying the boy who was killed lived not far from here though. Penworth."

Penworth? An image of Mikey's face flashes through my mind. Suddenly, my legs feel like jelly.

Mum is worried now. She puts her hand on my arm.

"Matt, love, you look very pale. Go and sit down. I'll bring you a drink and you can have one of the cakes I've made."

"Yeah," I say, "I think I'll do that. Thanks, Mum."

Mum heads for the kitchen and I take my coat off.

As I'm hanging my coat up on the pegs, I see myself in the mirror. Mum's right. I look pale. In fact, I'm as white as a sheet. The house is warm, but I'm shivering. It's like the cold has seeped right into my bones. I go into the front room. Sinking onto the sofa, I pick up the remote.

The TV flickers into life. I go up and down the channels, looking for something to watch.

There's a football match on Sky, but it's nobody good. The scores from earlier today are scrolling along the bottom of the screen. Renton United got a draw away at Letchford.

I change over to BBC One. It's the local news. The stabbing in Renton is the top story. The reporter is a bloke with ginger hair, wearing a grey overcoat and a black scarf. He's near the bus station. Behind him, people have already started laying flowers.

BREAKING NEWS STABBING
FATAL STABBING OF TEENAGE BOY IN RENTO

Two girls are standing side by side, crying. It seems strange. Unreal. I was there myself, less than an hour ago.

Now the newsreader is going through the details of what's happened. The stabbing. The attacker getting away. The police asking for anyone who might have seen anything to come forward. The victim. Seventeen years old. A promising footballer.

I feel like there's an icy hand closing tightly around my heart. I shut my eyes. I know what I'm going to see when I open them. And I'm right.

The dead lad's face, staring back at me from the screen. It's a school photo, taken a couple of years ago. A smiling teenager in a blue blazer. But there's no mistaking who it is. Even without the scar on his cheek, or the gold earring.

His name is Michael Todd.

But I knew him as Mikey.

45

Reader challenge

Word hunt

1. On page 4, find an adjective that means "droopy".

2. On page 27, find a word that means "someone who tells on somebody".

3. On page 42, find a verb that means "soaked".

Story sense

4. How does the picture on page 37 show how Matt's mother is feeling?

5. Why does Matt try to keep his voice steady when talking to Mum? (page 40)

6. Why does Matt go pale when Mum says the boy lived in Penworth? (page 40–41)

7. What does Matt mean when he says, "I feel like there's an icy hand closing tightly around my heart"? (page 44)

8. What do you now think happened to Matt when he was on the bus?

Your views

9 Did you enjoy the story? Give reasons.

10 At what point in the story did you work out how Mikey was involved with the stabbing? What clues were given in the text or the pictures?

Spell it

With a partner, look at these words and then cover them up.

- drumming
- stabbing
- spinning

Take it in turns for one of you to read the words aloud. The other person has to try and spell each word. Check your answers, then swap over.

Try it

With a partner, imagine you are miming the scene between Matt and Mikey on the bus. Start with Mikey sitting down and end when he gets off the bus. Make your actions reflect Matt's changing feelings and what you now know about Mikey's situation.

William Collins's dream of knowledge for all began with the publication of his first book in 1819. A self-educated mill worker, he not only enriched millions of lives, but also founded a flourishing publishing house. Today, staying true to this spirit, Collins books are packed with inspiration, innovation and practical expertise. They place you at the centre of a world of possibility and give you exactly what you need to explore it.

Collins. Freedom to teach.

Published by Collins Education
An imprint of HarperCollins*Publishers*
77–85 Fulham Palace Road
Hammersmith
London
W6 8JB

Browse the complete Collins Education catalogue at **www.collinseducation.com**

This book is dedicated to Carey, Alex, Lily, Mum and Dad
Text © Dan Tunstall 2012
Illustrations by Andrew Bock © HarperCollins Publishers Limited 2012

Series consultants: Alan Gibbons and Natalie Packer

10 9 8 7 6 5 4 3 2
ISBN 978-0-00-746478-4

British Library Cataloguing in Publication Data.
A catalogue record for this publication is available from the British Library.

Commissioned by Catherine Martin
Edited and project-managed by Sue Chapple
Illustration management by Tim Satterthwaite
Proofread by Grace Glendinning
Design and typesetting by Jordan Publishing Design Limited
Cover design by Paul Manning

Acknowledgements

The publishers would like to thank the students and teachers of the following schools for their help in trialling the Read On series:

Southfields Academy, London
Queensbury School, Queensbury, Bradford
Langham C of E Primary School, Langham, Rutland
Ratton School, Eastbourne, East Sussex
Northfleet School for Girls, North Fleet, Kent
Westergate Community School, Chichester, West Sussex
Bottesford C of E Primary School, Bottesford, Nottinghamshire
Woodfield Academy, Redditch, Worcestershire
St Richard's Catholic College, Bexhill, East Sussex